YIKES, Stinkysaurus!

Pamela Butchart
& Sam Lloyd

BLOOMSBURY
LONDON   NEW DELHI   NEW YORK   SYDNEY

The dinosaurs were scary!
Some had **big** sharp claws.

Some had horns and spiky tails,
and some had giant jaws!

T-rex had a temper,
and Bronto sure was tall.

Raaah!

But **Stinkysaurus** was, by far, the scariest of them all!

YIKES, STINKYSAURUS!

The dinos rushed for cover,
when **Stinkysaurus** was about!

He smelled so bad that just one whiff,
could knock a T-rex out!

This great big grubby giant,
refused to take a bath.
So everywhere he roamed,
he left a **stinky** muddy path.

Stinkysaurus was a snot beast.
He loved to sneeze...

ATCH-OOO!

He splattered all the dinos,
in yucky, sticky goo!

He never **ever** brushed his teeth,
so his breath was super-grotty.
And, poo! You won't believe the smells,
that parped out from his botty!

"Enough!" said Triceratops.
"We've got to get him clean."

So the dinos made the **biggest** bath, anyone had **ever** seen.

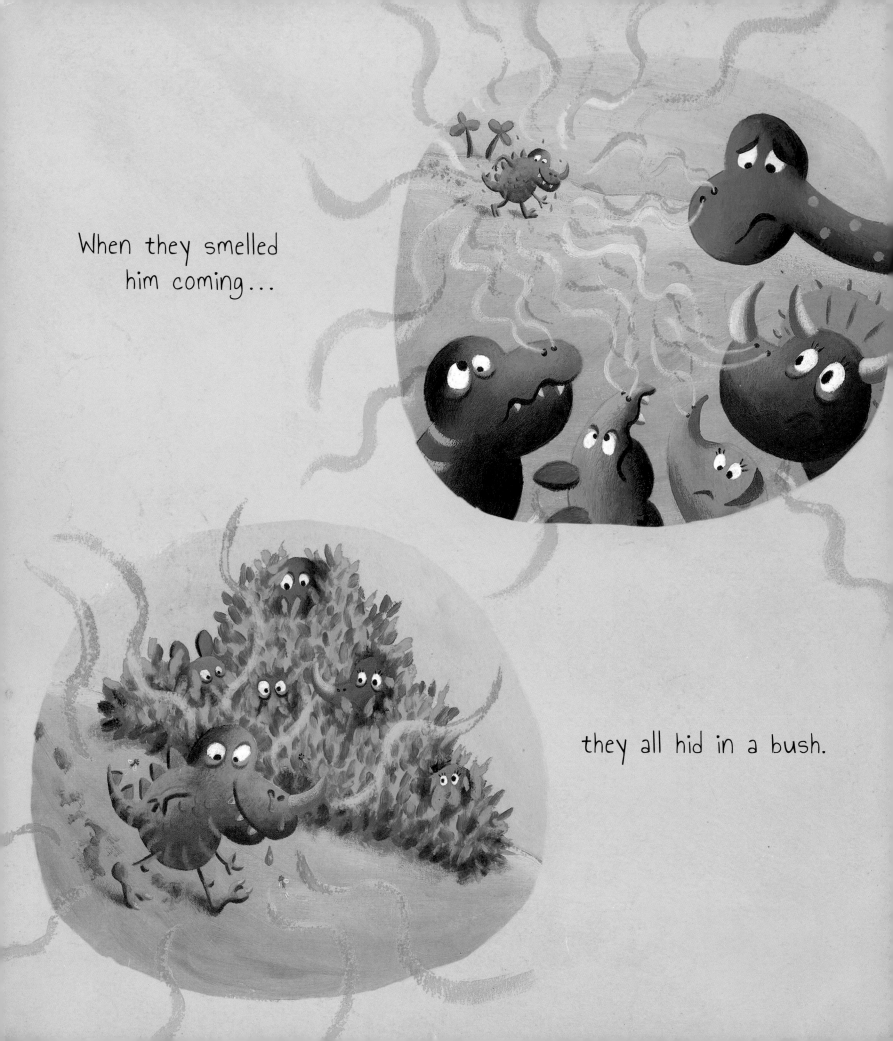

When they smelled him coming...

they all hid in a bush.

Then when he wasn't looking, they gave a great big...

PUSH!

Stinkysaurus shone and gleamed, as clean as clean could be.

"You're not so scary any more," the dinos cheered with glee!

Stinkysaurus felt fantastic, when no one ran away.

He'd finally found some dino friends,
who wanted him to play.

So now when **Stinkysaurus**
jumps in the swamp...

Because his friends all jump in too!

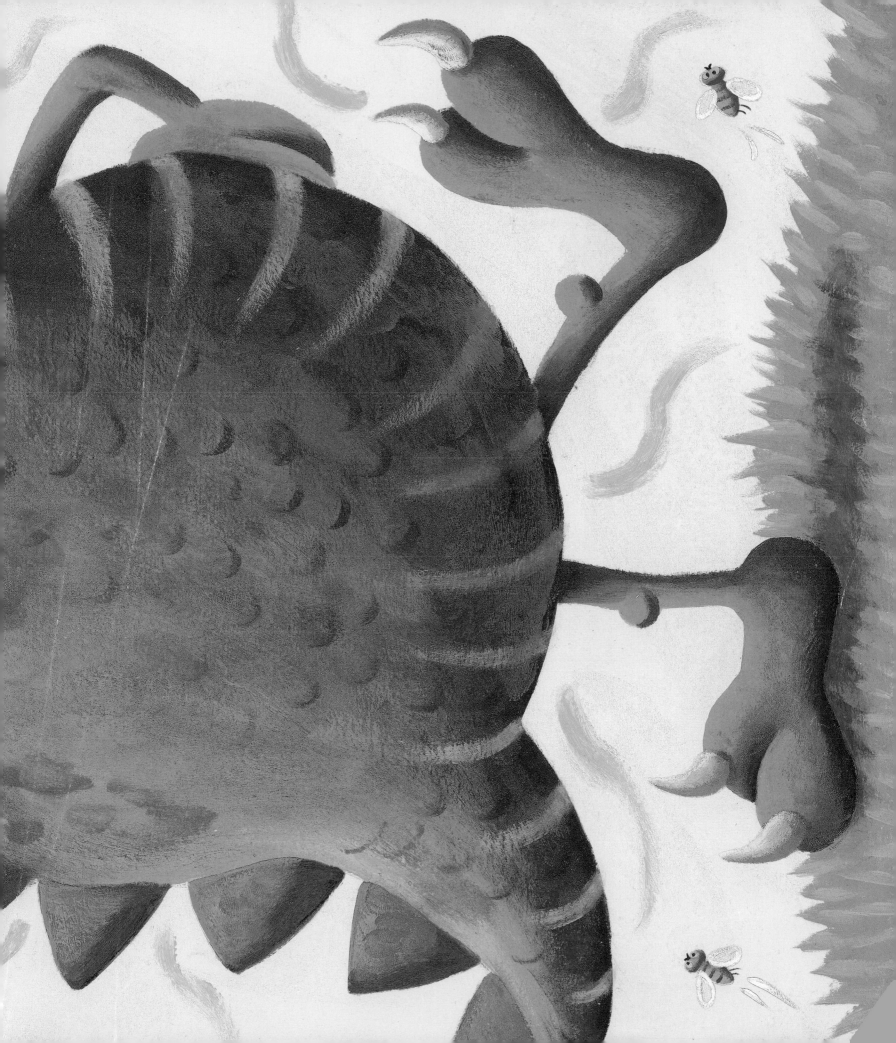

For Andysaurus, with love.
With thanks to Becky and Emma. ~ PB

For the cool kids, and super staff at
Carlton Hill Primary School, Brighton ~ SL

Bloomsbury Publishing, London, New Delhi, New York and Sydney

First published in Great Britain in 2014 by Bloomsbury Publishing Plc
50 Bedford Square, London, WC1B 3DP

Text copyright © Pamela Butchart 2014
Illustration copyright © Sam Lloyd 2014
The moral rights of the author and illustrator have been asserted

A CIP catalogue record for this book is available from the British Library

ISBN 978 1 4088 3706 1 (HB)
ISBN 978 1 4088 3707 8 (PB)
ISBN 978 1 4088 3967 6 (eBook)

Printed in China by C & C Offset Printing Co Ltd, Shenzhen, Guangdong
1 3 5 7 9 10 8 6 4 2

www.bloomsbury.com